OUT OF THE BLUE TRUTH

BRISIBE TAMARAUEKIYE

ISBN: 9798843866716

Cover design by: Art Painter
Library of Congress Control Number: 2018675309
Printed in the United States of America

This book is dedicated to God almighty who has been my source of inspiration.

CHARACTERS

Esther
Alakemefa----------------------------------Esther's Mother
Oweilaemi----------------------------------Esther's Father
Finine--Esther's Friend
Timipere-------------------------------------Esther's Friend
Doubra------------------------------------- Student
Ebitimi--Doubra's Mother
Olotuowei---------------------------------Doubra's Father
Paibi--Doubra's Friend
Noel--A businessman
Doctor
Nurse
Pastor Ebikeme
Congregation
Kidnappers
Prisoners
D.P.O.
Police Constable
F.R.S.C. Officer
Alakemefa's neighbors
Ambulance Officers

PROLOGUE

Spotlights revealing Narrator on stage. He bows and assumes his position, then faces the audience with a beaming ecstatic expression.

Narrator: [Showcasing] The play starts with rainstorms. It is in the early hours of Friday morning, the clock reads 5:05 AM. The morning is windy. There's a chill in the air. A stiff breeze blows; suddenly storm clouds cover the sky, then the rain begins. At first, the rain pours down in round drops and gradually changes into sheets. The wind whistles, a storm strikes, there is a flash of lightning and a clap of thunder. Hmm, just keep your fingers crossed in anticipation of what this full of suspense drama will unfold. [Narrator exits]

ACT ONE
Scene One

[Scene is Oweilaemi's sitting room. Esther enters. She is dressed in a flannel nightgown; pacing around the sitting room, she looks puzzled, pondering over her parent's business trip.]

Esther: [Talking slowly] My God, this is way getting out of hand. I don't understand what's going on? My parents were supposed to come back on Tuesday this week. What must have gone wrong? [She hears a knock on the entrance door.] Who's it?

Noel: It's me Esther, please open the door.

Esther: I can't recall your voice, the name please? [She reluctantly moves toward the door.]

Noel: It's Noel, your friend as well as your next-door neighbor. Please open the door.

Esther: I will be right out. [Opens the door and stares at him with cold eyes.] Don't stand outside shivering, come inside and get warm!

Noel: [Steps into the sitting room. He walks with quick light steps.] It's absolutely freezing outside. I'm freezing! [He sits on the couch. He's icy cold and thoroughly drenched.] It was really cold outside.

I went through hell.

Esther: [In amazement] what happened?

Noel: The rain ravaged my apartment roof. Especially my bedroom. To sum up, my house isn't conducive to stay for the main time. That's the reason I came here. When the rain stops, I will go back and fix things up.

Esther: That's bad. Um, it was the thunder rumbles that woke me up from sleep. Since then, there is no flicker of sleep in my eyes. [Heading to the kitchen] can you imagine that my parents are not yet back from their business trip and both their cell phones are switch off. There's no way to reach them. [Esther exits]

Noel: [unbuttons his wet shirt and hangs it on the rocking chair behind him. Water slightly drizzles on the tiles from the wet shirt. Esther returns shortly with a cup of tea and hands it to Noel. He grabs the cup of tea with a smile] thank you.

Esther: You're welcome. [She is pretty carried away by Noel's six-pack and promptly comes back to her senses. She sits next to him.] How do you feel now? Is the cold still that intense?

Noel: [Fixes his gaze on her] I'm perfectly good now! [Demonstrating] you, sitting next to me in a moment like this, is like I'm in paradise, rejoicing with the angels for sending such a beautiful soul on this earth, and fortunately enough, she is right here staring at my face.

Esther: [Laughs out loud] you are funny! [Overwhelmed with excitement.] Oh my gosh! Seriously, you're good at composing a poem. Your words had me in stitches.

Noel: [Happily] Thank you. OK! Let me give you stanza two.

Esther: [Chuckles]Oh yeah, I'm listening.

Noel: [Sighs heavily. He put down the tea glass on the table.] Oh! What a great moment! Actually, the worth of money cannot be compared to the love I have for you. The love I'm incubating in my heart for you can calm the violent waves of the sea. My priceless jewel, why not give me a chance? I would prove to you that you worth my love. Heavens bless the day you were brought to this world. Only your smile can ease one's high temper! Please, just give me the chance.

Esther: [Looks blank] You must be living in a dreamland if you think that I will give you the chance you're in quest of. [Tired exhales] look, I would've love to give you that chance but unfortunately, I'm in a committed relationship. I have told you a couple of times. Why do you keep pestering me?

Noel: [Looking more serious and feels disappointed. Holds her hands tenderly and stares into her eyes; trying to maintain eye contact, with a soft voice.] Esther, look me in the eye. You know, today isn't the first time I'm expressing my mind to you that I do love you. I am not disputing the fact that you've got a boyfriend but why not.....

Esther: [Cuts in] my boyfriend has won my heart and my soul. I love him with every bone in me. I don't really know how to tell you this, He has changed my perception of relationships.

Noel: [folds his hands in astonishment] ehn eh!

Esther: He taught me what it means to truly love someone. Every moment we spend together is a treasured moment. It is like time stands still each time we are together.

Noel: Wow, that's true love.

Esther: [Her voice is pitch low] my relationship with my boyfriend is overwhelmed with feelings of piercing sweetness. And I don't want anything to come between us.

Noel: I do understand. [He holds her hands softly. His warm touch sends chills down her spine. He becomes emotional. Making her respond emotionally as well.] Babe! How I wish you can understand my feelings for you. I haven't madly fallen in love as I am at present. I am desperately in love with you. Do you believe in love at first sight? Right from the very day I set my eyes on you, there's this passion of love burning in my heart. You were the one that ignited it, no one else, and each time I see you, the flames keep increasing like whooshing flames. The heat is so intense that I'm getting out of control. My dear [He inhales and sighs slowly] the love I have for you is sincere and inexplicable. Please, don't let it melt my heart away. You're the only person that can quench this passion of love. Please give me a try and I shall be forever in your debt of love. I promise you I'm not going to pay you in dribs and drabs. I will pour out my whole heart of love for you.

[While Noel is expressing his feelings, Esther is extremely intoxicated by his soft voice. His tender hands gradually drifting to other parts of her body which ignites her emotions and she feels the warmth of his hands around her which spurs her to lose control. Noel couldn't resist the urge of making love to her. He gives her a cool kiss. Esther is still lost in raving emotions. His hands wandered through her body. He cupped her head in his hands and lowers his face until his lips crushed against hers. He pries her lips apart with his tongue and
claims her mouth, rolling his tongue around hers, his hands tangle in her hair, then running up and down her body. He cuddles her. Her arms encircling him, face buried against his chest. Esther at this point, couldn't resist the urge and pressure, absolutely carried away. Within a couple of minutes, they find themselves making love. Kissing passionately and sighing with pleasure.]

Esther: Oh my God! What have I just done? [Pushes Noel off her body.] Noel, what have you done to me? [Crying bitterly] Oh God! Have mercy on me! I plea for your mercy Lord! My whole life is in jeopardy now. Lord Jesus! please, forgive me-e-e-e-e!

Noel: [In a state of turmoil. His eyes glistening] that's ludicrous. I didn't force you.

Esther: I'm finished! I have lost my pride. My virginity! [Blood stains her nightgown and slides down to her legs.] All through my life, I've not indulged in this outrageous act. You have just deflowered me-e-e! [Crying aloud]

Noel: [Realizing that she was a virgin, becomes extremely happy and ready to love her passionately. He holds her softly, encircling his hands around her waist.] Esther, please I am sorry. [Trying to dry her tears] it hurts me so much to see you in tears. I promise I will make it up to you. You are the most beautiful girl I have ever seen. Yet, you were able to keep your virginity. What a virtuous girl you are with a distinctive personality! I promise to give You, my totality. I love you with my life, with every drop of blood that runs through my veins.

Esther: [Tearfully snaps herself from Noel's grip.] Behave yourself! For heaven's sake, leave me alone! Just let me be.

Noel: This is no time to be quarrelling. Don't be so noisy. I beg you. I assure you I will do my very best to take good care of you. I truly love you.

Esther: [Aggressively] Get out of my house and please do me the favour of never showing up again!

Noel: But babe, I'm... [Esther interrupts.]

Esther: Get out! Out of my house! [Noel takes his shirt and leaves.]

CURTAIN

SCENE-TWO

[The stage atmosphere looks so pure like a crystal. Birds are singing in the background. Depicting another new brand day. Doubra in a smart outfit comes to check on Esther. Doubra enters.]

Esther: [Lying on a two-seater sofa.] Hi love.

Doubra: Oh! you are up already, my love.

Esther: [Looks exhausted.] yeah!

Doubra: How did you sleep, my love? [He sits on the sofa and gasps.] Your face looks gloomy, is anything the matter?

Esther: Not really, is just that my night didn't go well.

Doubra: [Anxiously.] what happened?

Esther: Never mind, I'm OK.

Doubra: Are your parents back from their business trip?

Esther: Not yet [she murmurs] I am worried.

Doubra: [Places his right hand across her shoulder.] I guess they are doing good. You shouldn't be worried, OK? What do you care for breakfast? [Trying to brighten her day.]

Esther: [Gazes at him in amazement. A lovely smile curves her lips.] You mean, you want to prepare breakfast for me? [She smiles and caresses his cheek.]

Doubra: Yeah! [Excited, seeing the expression on her face changed. Do you like a sandwich and tea for breakfast?

Esther: Sure!

Doubra: Good! [Exclaimed excitedly and heading to the kitchen.] I will be back in a jiffy. Lest I forget, [He retraces his steps to give her a peck on the cheek and heads to the kitchen.]

Esther: I can't just wait to eat the breakfast that's specially prepared by my prince charming! [Esther's phone rings] Hello! Who is it?

Alakemefa: Esther my love! How good to hear your voice!

Esther: [surprised.] Mum!

Alakemefa: I truly miss you, my dear daughter.

Esther: Same here mum! Mum, how is daddy?

Alakemefa: He's fine. He's also longing to hear your voice.

Oweilaemi: My beautiful daughter, how are you doing?

Esther: I'm doing great dad.

Oweilaemi: We miss you, dear. I'm really happy to hear your voice.

Esther: Same here dad. Dad, why is it that you and mom's phones were not reachable. I was seriously worried. [She clears her throat and teases] you both are still having fun in Dubai, I guess?

Oweilaemi: Far from it.

Esther: Then why is it that you both haven't come back from your business trip?

Oweilaemi: It's a long story, my daughter. We were robbed.

Esther: Robbed? Oh my God!

Owailaemi: The good thing is we were able to buy the gold and keep them in the custody of our customer before the incident occurred. The robbers made away with our phones and every money we were left with. That is why we couldn't reach you on time. We were so fortunate to locate a good friend of mine yesterday who is residing here in Dubai. He helped us with a certain amount of money, so we're coming back to Nigeria today.

Esther: Dad I'm so sorry. I didn't know you were robbed.

Owailaemi: It's okay. I want you to cook my favourite meal.

Pulou-fiyai and Osun. I love the way you cook it. You know I miss our local delicacies.

Esther: [Laughing] I will dad, bye! Doubi love!

Doubra: [From the kitchen] yes, my love! I'm coming, just give me five minutes. [After a short while, Doubra enters.]

Esther: You won't believe that my parents just called.

Doubra: Really?

Esther: Yeah! They are coming back today.

Doubra: [Smiling] Wow! That's good. You look more beautiful when you smile. [Esther chuckles] yeah, it brings out the real beauty in you. [Doubra smiles warmly as he sits down and nestles against her.
Looking into her eyes.] I love looking into your eyes always because they are the window to your soul, and your soul is pure and beautiful.

Esther: You never cease to be funny. [Resting her head on his shoulder] I will love you till trees stop growing in the forest.

Doubra: [Laughing] Your voice sounds so lovely. I do love you more than words can express. Okay, let me go and finish up with the sandwich and the cup of tea that I was preparing for you. [He dashes off to the kitchen.]

CURTAIN

SCENE THREE

[Esther dresses with casual elegance. In a white top, blue jeans, and a pair of blue sneakers to match. Heading to school, she has already walked half a mile when Noel calls her.]

Noel: Esther please wait! [He hastens his steps to catch up with her. She doesn't slow her strides until he is face to face with her.] So good to see you! I'm sincerely sorry about what happened the other day. It was never my intention to offend you.

Esther: Umm, [she murmurs as her lip quivers and then her heart starts to beat more quickly as memories of how she lost her virginity to him stir up. She tries to talk to him but the rhythms of her breathing become intense.]

Noel: Why do you get so nervous? See, you can rely on me for anything you want. I love you more than the world itself! Every time I see you, you take my breath away. I do love you and I'm ready to do anything for you. I promise you; I will show you a life of affluence and adventure.

Esther: [Looking furious] Are you done with your annoying words? What are you babbling about?

Noel: It isn't worth quibbling over such a minor issue. [A feeling of guilt begins to stir in him.]

Esther: [Sorrowfully] Did you know that you render my life miserable? My whole life is in jeopardy because of you. Do you realize the situation you got me into? [She sadly leaves]

Noel: But babe! My love for you is real. You're going to forget about this. [He feels no remorse about her sadness. Esther is out of sight and Noel exits.]

CURTAINS

ACT TWO SCENE ONE

[Timipere's room. The room is quite messy. The bed is rumpled. Shoes and books are jumbled together on the floor. The room is decorated in such a fashion to exhibit a student's room. She's eating breakfast when Noel enters.]

Timipere: Hey, Noel! [The aroma of the rice and scrambled eggs wafting into his nostrils.] What a surprise visit!

Noel: Wow! [Exclaims slowly.] I'm starving already. The aroma of the rice is smelling so good!

Timipere: Would you like to eat? [Putting on a vague smile.]

Noel: You've almost finished the rice. [Jokingly] me, I can eat o!

Timipere: It's a normal thing for you guys na.

Noel: [sits on the bed.] My people say a man wey sabi eat, him go dey take good care of him wife. Guys are supposed to eat well o, so that we go dey get strength provide food for the family.

Timipere: [Laughs shortly] I hear you, Sir! [Both laugh]

Noel: On a more serious note, I'm here to discuss a very crucial matter with you.

Timipere: Crucial matter?!

Noel: Yes! I am terribly serious. [He leans forward and sighs slowly.]

Timipere: I am all ears.

Noel: It's about your friend Esther.

Timipere: What's going on between you two?

Noel: I'm madly in love with her.

Timipere: [Jokingly] I can see two love birds.......

Noel: [Cuts in] This is no time for jokes. I'm definitely serious. I have made a strenuous effort to express the depth of my love to her but she always turns me down. She is an ineluctable part of my life that I cannot let go of so easily. She is breathtakingly beautiful. The gentle curve of her lips when she smiles pierces my heart like a spear fashioned out of pure light. Her eyes are so pure, they are like another kind of light. Whenever I hear her speak, her angelic voice always sweeps me off my feet. Her flaming hair is like the sun turning into smoky brass under a night sky. Her ebony skin, her rosy-tantalizing lips, her shapely figure, her straight-long legs, everything about her is beautiful. Each passing day, I'm longing to feel the warmth of her hands on my beating heart. I want her to take me into her loving arms. My heart is panting for her love.

Timipere: En-eh! This is serious. You are deeply in love o! How can I be of help to you?

Noel: A lot! See, [He fixes his gaze on her more closely] If you can convince her to fall in love with me; I assure you, I have a lot of surprise packages for you. I will also give you some incentives.

Timipere: Surprise package?! That's cool! But the problem is, she's deeply in love with a guy named Doubra and their relationship is gradually leading to marriage.

Noel: What did you just say? Marriage?!

Timipere: Do you really have no idea about their relationship?

Noel: [Slightly annoyed] That guy is such a pain in the neck. Esther told you that? That her relationship with Doubra is advancing to marriage? [In disbelief] No, no, you're exaggerating.

Timipere: Why the long face? Come on, don't keep up with that. I promise you; as far as the surprise packages coupled with the incentives are available, I'm at your service 24/7.

Noel: Great! [Flickers a smile.] That's completely noble. I want you to snap to it.

Timipere: A-a-h! That will be a snack. [Smiles] It's very easy to convince Esther. I will get in touch with her and give you the feedback.

Noel: [Glances at his wristwatch.] Gracious me! I have to go before my supplier looks for me. I really had a swell time with you. See you later. [He leaves.]

SCENE TWO

[Inside the university campus, there's an open eatery where students troop in to eat.

Timipere and Finine are sitting on plastic chairs at a corner in the eatery, chatting.]

Timipere: [Calls out] Finine! Hmm, guess who Noel is crushing on?

Finine: You know I'm not good at guessing. Just tell me.

Timipere: It's Esther. He is terribly in love with her.

Finine: [Surprised.] You've got to be kidding me!

Timipere: No! I kid you not. I'm serious.

Finine: That guy na big catch o! He has a big electronic store in Bomadi market.

Timipere: Enhh! [In astonishment] Are you for real? [She calls for the waiter and the waiter walks in.]

Waiter: What can I get you?

Timipere: [To Finine] what do you care for?

Finine: Hmm, [contemplating] I only have time for a snack. Do you sell snacks?

Waiter: Yes ma!

Finine: Okay. [Trying to sit up properly.] Burger and Fanta will just be fine.

Timipere: All right then, bring two burgers, a Fanta and a Coke. [The waiter leaves] Esther is so fortunate.

Finine: But wait o! How did you know about Noel's interest in Esther? [She shows concern.] Did Noel tell you that?

Timipere: He came to my house yesterday and expressed his innermost feelings to me; how he loves her and wants her by all means. [Demonstrating with her hands.] You know what? He said that if I can convince her, he has a surprise package for me attached with some incentives.

Finine: Wow! That's divine! But wait o! Do you realize that Doubra and Esther are deeply in love? Their love waxes stronger with the years. And from the look of things, they might get married in the near future.

Timipere: [Cheerfully] Hey, what's wrong with that? I Just want our friend to be on the right track. You know, that boy Doubra is a medical student and he does not have much money to take good care of our friend. 90% of his income goes to his academic expenditures. Here's a golden opportunity for our friend to step into a life of luxury. Lest I forget, weren't you the one who told me earlier that he has a big electronic store in the Bomadi market? [The waiter enters. She gently places the tray containing the items on the table and leaves.

Timipere reaches for the key holder on the table and opens her coke with it, followed by Finine and they both eat.]

Finine: Babe! Let us be honest, you don't care about her feelings. Do you?

Timipere: Yes of course, I do care about her feelings. Esther na correct babe wey be sey I no want any bad thing to happen to her.

Finine: [Chuckles] True love conquers everything. [Esther comes striding along to meet them.] See who is coming.

Timipere: [Excited] Wow! Here comes the most beautiful girl in the whole wide world!

Esther: [Smiling] bad girls! [She taps both Timipere and Finine on the shoulders playfully.] You guys dey chill for here ona no even fit call me abi? [They both laugh]

Finine: We are just passing time here o! [Esther sits down] We are indeed having a great time here.

Timipere: You care for a drink?

Esther: Yes O! I seriously need a drink to calm down my brain. The sun glared down at me relentlessly from the sky.

Timipere: [Teasing] Ajebota! [To the waiter] hello, Madam! [The waiter enters] get her burger and Pepsi. I know, she likes Pepsi a lot.

Esther: [chuckles] naughty girl! Em, were you in the last class? I didn't see you guys. As in enh, the class was fun. Dr. Patrick was cracking us up with his funny talks.

[Enters the waiter. She places the items on the table and leaves.] Thank you, dear. You girls are keepers!

Timipere: [Smiling] you are welcome. [Esther opens the Pepsi and sips it.] Esther, Noel does love you.

Esther: Hunh! [The expression on her face changes.] What's this about? Is it an interrogation or a bit of advice? Wait for a second, how did you know? Did he tell you anything?

Finine: [Teases] Babe, chill! Just listen to what she has to say.

Timipere: Actually, [sighs] ehm, he expressed his feelings to me that he does love you. [Timipere reaches out her right hand to tap

Esther affectionately on the shoulder but Esther dodges it.] Noel is a nice guy. He's basically Like the cutest being in the world. He's handsome, tall, virile, and has the money to take good care of you.

Esther: Why didn't I expect less from you? Believe me, I'm not in any way interested.

Timipere: Don't get it twisted. I'm in no way forcing you to date Noel.

Finine: Esther, Timipere is right. Noel is a nice guy every girl is craving to date. Here's a golden opportunity for you. Don't let it go in vain. Make hay while the sun shines. Wake up, babe! Wake up! This is a huge opportunity. You need to utilize it appropriately. The icing on the cake is he has a clean Benz coupled with an ample electronic store. You know that. The guy is desperately in love with you. He'll change your world. You will live a life of luxury and ease.

Esther: [Slightly angry] I don't want to jump down somebody's throat. So, for the love of God, I beseech you, suspend this topic. I prefer not to talk about it. I don't have the strength to go through it because I don't have that luxury of time. I have more important things to focus my energy on.

Timipere: I know it seems trivial to you but we just want to give you a thousand reasons to be happy. It's all in the bit to make your life comfortable.

Esther: [Exhales heavily] Please fix it at the back of your mind that I love Doubra with the whole of my being. He's the crown of my heart and I love every bit of him.

Timipere: You know he's a medical student and all his income flows into his school expenditures.

Esther: [Furiously] Gosh! You guys are being annoying. Tell me you two are not a killjoy [She gets up and leaves]

Timipere: [Shakes her head] poor girl, I feel sorry for her. [She stands up] I'm running late. [She calls the waiter's attention and the waiter walks in.] What's the amount to be paid?

Waiter: Everything amounts to #1,000 (one thousand naira.)

Timipere: [Reaches into her purse and picks #1,000 naira note.] Here is your money. [Both Timipere and Finine leave.]

CURTAIN

SCENE THREE

[Scene is Noel's sitting room. The sitting room is arranged in such a lovely fashion. Noel is sitting on a chair, surfing the internet with his smartphone. Timipere and Finine enter.]

Noel: Hey, Timipere what's up?

Timipere: I am good.

Noel: [Leaps up and gives them a warm hug.] How fortunate you guys are. I was about to step out.

Timipere: Seriously! [She eases herself into a chair.]

Noel: Finine, it's been a while. How is school? [Offering her a chair.]

Finine: Fine! [Teasingly] you look charming.

Noel: [Smiles] thank you. What can I offer these two beautiful damsels? Do you like Hollandia yogurt?

Timipere: Yep! I know Finine will like it. [Jokingly] You like Hollandia yogurt, don't you?

Finine: [Smiling] Whatever.

Noel: [Brings out one Hollandia yogurt from his refrigerator, takes three plastic cups and pours some quantity of the content into their cups. Everybody sips]

Finine: This drink is really chill!

Noel: [Empties the content in his cup at once.] A-a-h! I love this drink!

Finine: Is it your favourite drink?
Noel: Yup! I like it a lot.

Timipere: Yeah, the drink is nice. It tastes good, hum Noel, I have discussed with Esther.

Noel: [Delightfully] Really! How did it go?

Timipere: Not so good.

Noel: [The expression on his face changes from one of happiness to one of anger and anxiety.] What do you mean?

Esther: All efforts to convince her proved abortive. I wasn't the only one to let her know how you love her sincerely. Finine did her best as well but she didn't give us a listening ear.

Noel: Bullshit! [Flinging his empty plastic cup away.] So, what do we do now?

Finine: Actually, Esther loves Doubra dearly and I suppose there's nothing you can do to alter her love for Doubra unless you halt their relationship.

Timipere: Truly, Esther is head over heels in love with her boyfriend. And her boyfriend, on the other hand, can't have an amazing day without having her by his side. They stick together like bread and butter. So, I guess, you better map out some strategies to win her love.

Noel: [Exceedingly angry.] Ehmm! That boy Doubra is in hot water. It's time to take the bull by the horn.

Finine: [Scoffs] You're speaking in parables. What are you up to?

Noel: [Emotionally] Would you believe your ears that I recently deflowered Esther? [Trying to be precise.] About five days ago. [Finine and Esther are incredulous at the news.]

Finine: [Highly skeptical] mi kpo egberi ke pei'a'sei! [Putting her two palms together.] I'm shocked to the core. Do you actually mean what you're saying? Because, the Esther, I know isn't capable of betraying her boyfriend, talk more of cheating on him. She doesn't seem like the infidelity type.

Timipere: So, you mean Esther and her boyfriend don't involve sexual activities in their relationship?

Finine: But how were you able to have your way in between her legs if truly she was a virgin!

Noel: Hum! It's a long story.

Timipere: [Enthusiastically] Explain it in a nutshell so that our doubt will be cleared.

Noel: To cut a story short, it was last week Friday morning, about a couple of minutes gone past five, it rained cats and dogs that very morning. It was storming all through. The storms ravaged my apartment roof. Due to that fact, I went to Esther's house for shelter. She told me that her parents went on a business trip. So, I expressed my heartfelt love to her and in that process, we found ourselves making love. From there I discovered that she was a virgin. That's why I'm like an infant who is always desirous for his mother's tender loving care.

Finine: This whole story sounds too complicated. Esther and Doubra have been dating for a long time and they haven't got it on but you were opportune to have a go at it.

Noel: Sounds unbelievable right? Maybe Doubra is a celibate. That notwithstanding, all I'm striving at is to pull her out of her boyfriend's grip. Let's put this into consideration, I assume we blackmail Esther by letting her know that if she doesn't comply with me, I will let that so-called Doubra know that she isn't any longer a virgin that I had deflowered her. What do you think?

Timipere: Sounds great! That does sort of ring a bell.

Finine: [Unhappy] you mean you want to play games on Esther? I'm not a party to this. Please absolve me from this obligation. I can't do such a thing for my own selfish interest.

Noel: [Encouraging Finine] Oh come on! Don't keep on with that. Try to understand me. [Impatiently] I'm in love with the first girl I ever had the privilege to deflower. She's mine. I assure you, if you back me up to execute this plan, I will surprise you with something good.

Timipere: [Gets up and stretches her body.] We got to go; we've overstayed. We have a lot to put in place today. I will see to what you've said. [Finine stands up and they both leave.]

ACT THREE

Scene One

[Inside Doubra's house, Esther and Doubra are having a nice time together, catching fun. Esther places her head on Doubra's chest. Zara Larrson's song, I can't fall in love without you is blazing in the background.]

Doubra: My love [Brisk silence] I want to make a request. [Smiling] and I don't want you to decline it. Can I let the cat out of the bag?

Esther: [Enthusiastically] you're keeping me in suspense. You know I can't decline any request from you. [She plants a kiss on his forehead.]

Doubra: Can you dance for me?

Esther: [Amazed] My goodness! Your request is breathtaking. Yes, of course, I can dance for you all day long, till evening welcomes the presence of the stars and the moon.

Doubra: [In excitement] That's my baby! [He stands up and holds her tight from behind and whispers into her ears.] Baby, I will love you until sugar becomes tasteless.

Esther: [Smiling] your fresh breath just caresses my face like a scented powder and your voice was like a soft feather that ran down my spine and up my body. My ears ache to hear your intoxicating voice always.

Doubra: [Laughs] really! Your voice also sounds like a bewitching musical instrument. Whenever you speak, your words flow like a slow dreamy melody.

Esther: [Smiles] You're kidding me! Okay, take your hands off me; let me dance for you.

Doubra: [Relinquishes his grip on her. Gets seated and watches her with rapt attention as she dances to the rhythms of the song.] Whoop! I never knew my love can dance this good. [He walks up to her, holds her by the hands, and they both dance slowly to the rhythms of the song amidst kissing. Esther's cell phone rings.] Who is this caller that wants to disrupt our happy mood? [Teasing] that person should have to wait na.

Esther: [Dips into her pocket and fetches out the phone.] Hello!

[Doubra gets back to his chair.]

Noel: Esther, if you know what's good for you, you better let me into your life and give me room to continuously make love with you, or else, I'll let your so-called Doubra know that you are no longer a virgin that I've deflowered you.

[Esther is speechless] you belong to me. You are mine! [She hangs up the call and slumps onto the chair closest to her. She is moved to tears.]

Doubra: [Worried] What happened? Did anything bad happen to either your parents or relatives? My love, please talk to me. [He becomes uncomfortable] you look tensed up. What is the matter?

[Esther is not speaking] come on, talk to me. What is it that you've bottled up?

Esther: You won't understand.

Doubra: Understand what? I don't get you.

Esther: It is a personal matter.

Doubra: [Not impressed with her reply.] Don't you know that your burden is my burden? Our relationship has grown past mere intimacy. Do you still have it at the back of your mind that we will get married very soon, as soon as I'm done with my school? [Pleading] please, it will do us no good to hide our burdens under the carpet. So, I prefer we should disclose our burdens to each other.

Esther: My love, it is obvious that we are building our relationship towards marriage. [Trying to cover herself up.] But it is not a necessity that I have to tell you every single thing I'm passing through because my mum once told me that I should learn how to tackle circumstances by myself so that when I'm no longer under their roof, I will be able to face the hurdles of life. [Stirring up a fake smile to convince Doubra.]

Doubra: No problem. Though you insist not to tell me. I do understand that your love for me is real and it will remain evergreen in my heart.

Esther: Thanks for understanding. [She feels relaxed.] I super love you, dearie! [She leans over to peck him on the cheek] I promise, my love for you will last like the sun.

SCENE TWO

[Doubra is heading to school. Putting on a lab coat because he is going to a practical class. Holding a writing pad and Biology practical manual in his right hand. He walks close to a lonely crossroad. A group of boys emerge from an unknown direction and round him up. All disguised their faces. Holding cutlasses, axe and a pistol. Within a twinkle of an eye, they start unleashing blows on him; blindfolds his eyes, fasten his mouth with a tape. Doubra is struggling to get loose from their grip. They take him to the stage. The stage is decorated in such a way as a jungle. Doubra tries to scream.]

Kidnapper 1: See this mumu o! watin dey do you? [Threatens him] If I land this cutlass on you ehn; your life will not remain the same.

Kidnapper 2: [Gives him a dirty slap on the face. Doubra groans heavily and sighs deeply.] sey bi you don kolo abi? Oya! Shout at the top of your voice. Make I see that savior wey go come help you escape. [He pushes him and Doubra sways.] make I see whether you go get wings fly from here to your so-called love. [He brings out a big rope and ties his wrists and legs.]

Kidnapper 1: [Lights a cigarette and puffs the smoke slowly on Doubra's face.] Sey you dey sow where you no go fit reap abi?

Kidnapper 3: You go die for love today. [Doubra fidgets. He tries to speak but his mouth is covered with tape.] Why did your Juliet never come to save you? [Doubra's cell phone rings. Kidnapper 1 dives into his front pocket and fetches out the phone, end the call, and slip it into his vest pocket.]

Kidnapper 4: Be like sey na him erema dey call o!

Kidnapper 3: This Abobi wan die for love. [Doubra struggles to escape. Both rain rapid blows on him.]

CURTAIN

SCENE THREE

[Esther is in her room looking miserable and anxious. Ruminating over Doubra's whereabouts.]

Esther: Where must he has gone to? This is the third day now and Doubra is nowhere to be found. His number isn't going through, hope all is well with him. [She tries to eat lunch but has no appetite.] Hoo! Where on earth is he that his phone isn't connecting? [She put across a call to Doubra's mother.]
Ma, has he come?

Ebitimi: My daughter, I'm seriously worried. [Crying through the phone.] This is making the third day now and my son is nowhere to be found. There's no glimmer of hope that at least one or two persons have set eyes on him. [Crying loudly through the phone.]

Esther: [Enveloped in sadness.] Ma, calm down. Nothing bad will happen to him. Ma, have you taken any steps?

Ebitimi: [Sobbing] Yes O! My daughter! I've informed the Police and they're investigating. My daughter, the last time I set my eyes on Doubra, He told me that he's late for class so he was in a hurry to catch up with the class. [Sobbing Increases.] Ene egren otubo eba de yooo! They've succeeded in taking away my pride! The one who gives me joy!

Esther: Ma, is okay. I'm coming over to your place. [Esther exits]

SCENE FOUR

[In the jungle, Doubra is still in the custody of the kidnappers. Blood is gushing from his nostril and glides down to soak his lab coat. He looks pale and motionless.]

Kidnapper 1: [To Head kidnapper] Omo! You sure sey life still dey this Abobi?

Head kidnapper: O boy that one no concerns us. We have done our clean job. If him don kpeme, na to dispose his corpse inside bush.

Kidnapper 2: [examines him gradually. Pushes his head back and forth. Doubra swoons.] Ooh boy eeeh! [He places his hands on his head.]

Kidnapper 3: [Lifts Doubra's hands and let go of them but there's no sign of consciousness.] Na true o!

Head kidnapper: [To Kidnapper 3] Untie him and unwrap the tape. [Kidnapper 3 starts to untie Doubra.] Get a sachet water and sprinkle it on him.

Noel: [Enters] Eh, what the heck is going on? [Doubra is lying lifeless on the ground.]

Head kidnapper: Guy, mellow down! I thought you said, you guys are no.1 enemies like cat and mouse. Here's an opportunity to take advantage of the girl. We did a clean job.

Noel: [Worried.] But I didn't say you should kill him.

Kidnapper 2: [Enters with a sachet water and drizzles it on Doubra. He gives him cardiopulmonary resuscitation. After series of efforts, Doubra sneezes, he looks absolutely worn to a frazzle.] A-ah! At last! He has regained consciousness.

Noel: [Relieved] Eh, young man! lookup. [Grabs Doubra cheeks with his thumb and first finger.] Stay away from Esther or else you will have yourself killed. Did you get it? [Doubra casts him a swift glance and realizes it's Esther's neighbor.] I say did you get it? [Doubra responds with a lift of his eyebrow.] Esther is mine! She's, my love. So, give her a distance. [He slaps him hard on the face.] If I see you anywhere around her, you're in my pot of soup. Is that clear? [Doubra nods in the affirmative.] Oya! Leave this place in the next 30 seconds. I can't stand your stinking sight. [Doubra leaves]

CURTAIN

SCENE FIVE

[In Doubra's family house. His mother is weeping bitterly. Moaning in despair. Esther is wrapped in thought. She tries to calm Ebitimi.]

Esther: You've been weeping for days. It's time you snap out of it.

Ebitimi: [Sobbing inconsolably] I wish I was dreaming. I want to wake up and realize all this was a dream.

Esther: [Soberly] Ma! If you continue in this state, it will certainly affect your health. Just put yourself together. Don't despair, God's help is on the way. I have this certainty that he's fine.

Ebitimi: [Tears streaming down her face]. After several years of toil and suffering in the university, is this how my son is going to end up? Oh, Temeowei! [Doubra enters. He looks extremely fatigued and pale. His lab coat soaked with blood.]

Esther: [Astonishingly] Doubra! [She jumps up and gives him a long hug amidst sobbing. His mother joins them.]

Ebitimi: [Tearfully] My son what happened? [She muddles in his appearance, She holds his reddish lab coat in amazement].

Esther: Ma, cheer up, tears are expressions of grief. Let's thank God for his infinite mercies, for bringing him back alive. Life is the most precious and greatest of all gifts.

Doubra: [Drops onto a chair feebly.] Esther! What relationship do you have with your next-door neighbor?

Esther: [Startled and dumbfounded.] Hmmm [her lip quivers.] What on earth are you talking about? What do you mean?

Doubra: I was kidnapped by your next-door neighbor. [Esther's heart beats faster. Ebitimi gasps, eyes wide in surprise.] He warned me to stay away from you because you're his girlfriend. He further threatened that if I don't keep my eyes off you, he will have me killed. [Ebitimi screams.] Please, can you tell me what is going on between you two?

Esther: [Tensed, shedding tears.] Truly, I don't have anything in common with that godforsaken Noel. In any case, he usually pesters me to date him but I resisted. [She wipes her eyes with a handkerchief.] I told him that I have you as my boyfriend.

Ebitimi: [Cuts in] but that hasn't gotten to the extent of kidnapping my son!

Doubra: [Stands up shakily, takes Esther by the hand, and stares raptly into her eyes.] My love! Put your worries behind and let's face up to the fact that Noel or whatever is an intruder in our lives and we must not allow him to ruin our relationship. [Gives her an affectionate kiss on the forehead.] I love you and I will always stand by you, come hell or high water, no matter what happens.

Ebitimi: [Angrily] look, either you call it love or not, I'm no longer in support of your relationship. From today henceforth, let this relationship cease to exist, or else I will create havoc and the result won't be positive to the both of you. [Ebitimi exits.]

Doubra: Never mind. Despite any circumstances we find ourselves in, I will still love you unconditionally.

Paibi: [Enters] My God in heaven! [Surprised.] Doubra! What happened to you? Where have you been all this while?

Doubra: My brother, it is a long story. I was kidnapped.

Paibi: [Astounded by the news of Doubra's kidnapped.] Jesus!

Doubra: I was in the custody of those repulsive kidnappers for three consecutive days without food and water.

Paibi: [Amazed] oh my goodness! That is astounding! But what have you done to deserve all this? Do they think you have a robust bank account?

Doubra: Robust bank account keh! I don't have even a dime in my account. My account is in the red. Do you know that Esther's next-door neighbour? [Paibi thinking] that tall guy who stays next to Esther's house.

Esther: His name is Noel.

Paibi: Oh my! [Nodding his head.] Yes! Yes!

Doubra: He is the brain behind this whole thing. He said I should back out of my relationship with Esther or else he will kill me. [Paibi gaps] I'm ready to fight him with my last breath.

Paibi: [one a mixture of wonderment and near astonishment] That guy is cruel and diabolic. How could he kidnap you because of a girl?

CURTAIN

ACT FOUR

SCENE ONE

[Scene is in Doubra's family sitting room. Doubra and his mother are playing Ludo. Having a nice time together. Noel and two policemen enter.]

Noel: It is that guy in white shorts sleeve, arrest him. [Pointing towards Doubra's direction.] You lunatic. You have the guts to tarnish my reputation. How dare you?

Ebitimi: [Confused] young man, what are you talking about. My son isn't known for crime.

Doubra: [Vexed] Mum! He was the one who hired boys to kidnaped me.

Police1: Shut up your frowzy mouth! If actually, he was the one who hired boys to kidnap you, where is your evidence to testify against him?

Doubra: Ehm, ehm! I was there all alone. [Ebitimi seizes Noel by the arm.] So, I only have God as my witness.

Noel: Woman! Get your filthy hands off me. [He pushes her and she booms on the floor. He denies the accusation leveled against him.] Your son here has tarnished my image. He Promulgated to the nooks and cranny of this city that I Noel, kidnapped him. Funny enough, because of one mere girl. Do you know how this accusation has affected me psychologically and otherwise? He defiled my reputation, woman!

Doubra: How dare you push my mother? [He lifts his right hand to dash him a slap but is held back by police1.]

Police 2: [Brings out his ID card] we are from Tuomo Police Division. In the absence of no evidence to validate the fact that it was Mr. Noel that kidnapped you, you're hereby under arrest for accusing an innocent man. Anything you say here will be used against you in the court of law. [Fear grips Doubra.]

Police 1: Mr. man! Common, stretch your hands. [Doubra reluctantly holds out his wrists so the policeman could fasten the handcuff. The police cuff him.]

Ebitimi: [Crying in terror.] My son didn't do anything wrong o! Mikpo akpo! [The policemen drag Doubra out of the house. Noel leaves.] My God will surely judge you. You kidnapped my son and still have the temerity to arrest him? You will not go scot-free. Remember; the eyes of the society are watching your actions.

CURTAIN

SCENE TWO

[Inside the prison, everybody is in a prison uniform. The prison president is giving Doubra a tough time.]

Prison President: Hey, come here! [Doubra stays on.]

Coward! Don't you have ears? Come here, my friend! [Doubra walks up to him. The President gives him a frog kick and a hard slap on the face, Doubra staggers.] Sebi you dey form strong boy abi? You no dey fear face abi. Mumu! No bi you I dey follow yan!

Doubra: What's wrong with you? How could you do that to me? [Boys round him up. His voice dwindles.] Why did you slap me?

Prison President: [Angrily] come on! Kneel, you dey speak English for me! You think sey na only you go school abi-e! Make I tell you, no be today wey I finish university. Ayebe! Fool common kneel down!

Doubra: [Mutters] but why?
Prison president: You're asking me why. Obey simple instructions. By the snaps of my fingers, I want to see you on the floor kneeling [Doubra reluctantly kneels] Introduce yourself.

Doubra: [Stutters] hum, ehm!
Prisoner 1: Speak up, mumu! [Both laugh scornfully.] Raise your

hands above your head and close your eyes. [He raises his hands and shuts his eyes.]

Doubra: Hmmm! My name is Olotuowei Doubra.

Prisoner 1: Wetin carry you come here, idiot?

Doubra: I'm a 400-level medical student. I'm in here because I was kidnaped by a guy called Noel due to the fact, he has an interest in my girlfriend and all his effort to win her love was to no avail. He's still the one who arrested me for tarnishing his image because I have no evidence to prove that he was the one that kidnapped me. [Couple of the prisoners moved with compassion.]

Prisoner 2: Presido, abeg free this guy so that he can have a stable mind to associate with us. The way him body dey shake, him fit die for fear.

Prisoner 3: Presido! I dey beg you too. This guy na innocent guy. See how sweat don cover him body. Make him no die for our hands. Only his voice self dey crack like CD plate way don spoil.

Prisoner 4: [Shoves off their plea.] Forget that one. That one na story way no get meaning. Him body just dey shake like fowl yansh. No be prison him dey? He has to be initiated into our association by giving him 10 lashes of the holy cane. [Doubra fidgets and starts begging the prison president.]

Prison President: Okay. Let's show him some love today because his case Is like out of the frying pan into the fire.

CURTAIN

SCENE THREE

[Outside Noel's house. Noel stepped off about ten strides from his house. He's heading to his electronic store. Esther suddenly appears and confronts him.]

Esther: How could you kidnap my boyfriend? [seizes his shirt firmly.] How dare you do such a dangerous thing to my boyfriend? Simply because I didn't succumb to your scandalous decision, right?

[Noel laughs hysterically.] Oh! Because I refuse to date you. In your wildest imagination, you think I will date you? [Putting her two palms together.] As if kidnapping him wasn't enough, you denied the fact that you masterminded his kidnap and went ahead to arrest him.

Noel: Are you done ranting? Your words are void of meaning. You're just wasting your precious time here. I will never let you be unless I have my way in between your legs once more. I've told you earlier that you belong to me. [He drags her to himself and scoffs.]

Esther: [Struggling to get free from Noel's grip.] Idiot! Let go of me! You can't fool me. You scallywag! Nothing in this world will compel me to date you because you're nothing but a devil.

Noel: [Laughing scornfully.] Oh! That's what you think? Ha, ha, I laugh at you. Have you forgotten your frustrating boyfriend behind bars? [He warns her.] If you don't comply with my demands, I will surely unveil to your so-called boyfriend in prison that I had deflowered you. [He giggles] and you know what? That means he will rot in jail with unavoidable emotions. Feeling being betrayed by his one and only girlfriend.

Esther: [On her knees, begging.] Please, for heaven's sake, don't disclose it to Doubra. It will subvert my relationship with him. I sincerely love him and I don't want anything to separate us neither any harm to come upon him. I beg of you.

Noel: Then simply comply. [He holds her right hand.] Esther, I need you in my life than I need water. I love you. I'm doing all this because I actually love you. [Esther snaps out her hand.] Just let go of that boy and step into a life of luxury.

Esther: It is not possible!

Noel: Then either you give me a chance to lie with you or you lose your darling boyfriend.

Esther: [Contemplating] I've heard you. I will give you a chance. But on one condition, it's on the basis that you will never reveal to Doubra that I'm no longer a virgin.

Noel: [Excited] good! Noted. [Esther leaves sadly. Noel exits.]

CURTAIN

SCENE FOUR

[In the sitting-room. Noel is sitting on a chair, chatting with Timipere.]

Noel: [Complementing Timipere] you look dazzling in your evening gown.

Timipere: [Smiling] thank you. Ehm, that reminds me. How far have you gone with Esther?

Noel: Very bad. She doesn't want me to date her but the good news is that she has agreed to sleep with me to die down the secret that she isn't a virgin.

Timipere: [Adding] Maybe she is gripped with the fear that Doubra will no longer marry her if he finds out that her body has been defiled. So, how do you intend to convince her?

Noel: Having you by my side, everything is at ease. I'm suggesting you should give her a call. Convincing her that you want to discuss a very delicate matter with her about her boyfriend and it is very urgent. Peradventure she comes, then we've hit the nail on the head.

Timipere: That's a nice strategy to lure her into your trap.

Noel: In a nutshell, I'm going to execute the plan in your house. Lest I forget, you have to give her a stipulated time.

Timipere: [Teasing] Remember she's still my friend and you have to take things easy. Oops! I shouldn't have said that.

Noel: Sure! Yeah, she's your friend.

Timipere: [Takes her cell phone, dials Esther's phone number.] Hello! Esther, you have to suspend whatever you're doing and come right away to my place. I want to tell you something very urgent. It pertains to Doubra, please come without delay. [Hangs up the call.]

Noel: That's a nice one. [Very happy, gives her a high five.] I never knew you're a genius! [Timipere smiling]

CURTAIN

SCENE FIVE

[Inside Timipere's house, Noel is eating boil plantain and vegetable sauce with Timipere, they are conversing when Esther enters. She couldn't believe her eyes. Seeing Noel in Timipere's house.]

Esther: I hope you don't mind me barging in like this?

Noel: You barged in on us while we are having a personal conversation.

Esther: [Feels miserable.] Oh, Pardon my manners. [She thinks.] What a mess have I gotten myself into? Noel is off-limit to me. Why is he here?

Timipere: [Marvels at the way Esther is standing and speechless.] What's the matter with you? Why are you standing like a statue? Help yourself to a chair.

Noel: Could you give us a moment alone.

Timipere: Noel! [Trying to be considerate.] Why this hostile attitude towards your neighbour? No, you can't make your hatred of her so obvious. She's still my friend. Remember!

Esther: [Realizes she is in a big mess and could see no way out. She tries to get out of the house in haste to be free from Noel's malicious behaviour.]
Just give me some minutes, I will be back shortly.

Noel: And where do you think you are going? Whether you like it or not, the right opportunity has come to execute what we agreed on. The choice is yours. Either you give me the chance or I tell your boyfriend what we did in the past. You know, it will ruin your relationship with your boyfriend.

Esther: [Blinks several times to stop the tears from forming in her eyes] Timipere, you deceived me! So your phone call wasn't real. I trusted you. You connived with Noel to play mischievous tricks on me. How could you?

Timipere: [Scoffs] don't get it wrong. [She sighs slowly] Am going to sound as calm as an evangelist. See, you are still my friend no matter what. I intend no harm. Let me tell you one vital thing you're yet to know. A broken relationship is better than a broken marriage. I advise you better forget about Doubra entirely and stick to Noel. Doubra is in prison suffering because his mother can't afford to bail him out. If you happen to marry Doubra, you will definitely suffer because his family is in a state of abject poverty. I mean they're living in penury. Be wise! A word is enough for the wise. I truly care about you and I don't want you to make the wrong decision in life.

Esther: [Gets mad at Timipere and in total disbelief of what her friend is capable of.] It hurts me so much that my own friend and my neighbour are capable of doing all these bad things against me. You guys did not only ruin my life but that of my love. [To Timipere] I thought you are a true friend. The friend I treasured so much has become a total stranger. [Sobbing] A true friend is supposed to stick closer than one's skin but the reverse is the case. What have I done to deserve all these wilful acts? You guys should get out of my life!

Noel: [Chuckles] you are not serious. See, there's no point crying over spilled milk or holding unto what was lost. It's time to let go. I have said it earlier, either you comply with my demand or you ruin your relationship. If you succumb to my demand, then I will never show up to disturb your peace again. [Timipere leaves to give them some privacy. Noel quickly shut the door and stands behind it.]

Esther: Hell knows I won't give in. Not even in my wildest dreams! You better open this door before I do anything funny. [She tries to get out but Noel overpowers her.] Leave me alone! Just let me be.

Noel: Until the needful is done before I will open this door. [Esther is pleading with Noel to change his mind.]

Esther: Please, I beg of you. Just let me go. [Kneels, pleadingly.] Please, please!

Noel: You're just wasting your time pleading. My mind is made up. [He walks up to her and holds her by the hands tightly.] There is nothing you will do that can make me change my mind.

Esther: [Realizing there's no way out to escape from the ugly situation she's into.] Okay, [crying] I have agreed. Please be fast, let me leave this lousy place.

CURTAIN

ACT FIVE
Scene One

[Oweilaemi is in the sitting room watching his TV show. Esther emerges from her room and sits next to her dad. She looks unhappy. Doubra in prison depressed her. Her mother walks in.]

Alakemefa: Esther, you still haven't eaten your dish of fried rice I served at the dining long ago. [She caresses her cheek gently.] My princess, you look depressed, is anything the matter? What is it you want to let off your chest? Tell me.

Esther: Mum, it is about Doubra. I'm worried about him. He's not safe in that horrible place. He's my husband to be and I ought to get him out of prison.

Alakemefa: We understand, but you need to eat so that you will be in good health.

Esther: [Calls out her dad.] Dad! Please, [she kneels on the floor opposite her dad.] Dad please, I want you to do me a favour to bail out Doubra from prison. He's been in prison for a couple of weeks now. He's passing through excruciating pain and agony. Dad, [pleadingly] I terribly need your help. Only you can help me out.

Oweilaemi: [Moved with compassion. Holds her by the hands and helps her to stand up.] I've heard you. I know Doubra is a nice boy, hardworking, intelligent, and God-fearing. I also know how much you love him. There is an Ijaw adage that says that kala tubo bra sorou dedaba okosu keme'mo Kere eyefede. (When a child knows how to wash his hands properly, he can dine with elders.) Doubra is such type. And such a kind of husband is rare to find. So, first thing tomorrow morning, I will go and bail him out of prison. I assure you.

Esther: [Feels elated and excited. She screams with joy.] Wow! You're the best dad in the world! [She gives him a long hug.] I love you, Daddy! You light up my life.

Oweilaemi: I love you too, daughter.

Alakemefa: [Smiling] I can see how happy you are. It's been ages since I've seen you this happy.

Esther: Yeah, yeah! Mum, I'm so happy. I can see you smiling too. [Alakemefa laughs softly.] Mum, where is my food? I've regained my appetite. Right now, I can even consume two plates of the fried rice. [Jokingly] I hope the chicken is big?

Alakemefa: [Chuckles] in case you care for chi exotic juice, check the refrigerator. I guess it will do you a lot of good to wash your food down with a chilled chi exotic juice.

Esther: Okay mum. [Oweilaemi laughing] dad, why are you laughing?

Oweilaemi: Your mum just made me take a trip down memory lane. [Laughing] when your mother was your age ehn, oh my goodness! She can eat!

Alakemefa: [Teasing] Hey, hey, don't tell lies. Have you forgotten how you almost finished a pot of rice when you were much younger?

Esther: [Laughing seriously] dad and mum, both of you are funny. Dad, is it true what mum just said?

Oweilaemi: Never mind, she's just kidding. [Smiling] I can barely finish a plate of rice. [He winks at Esther.] You know na.

Esther: Daddy I agree with you. [She leaves to the dining room.] Let me go and enjoy.

CURTAINS

SCENE TWO

Alakemefa is in the parlour, doing house chores. Holding a hand towel. She dusts the standing fan, cleans the TV, decoder, home theatre, and furniture. Her cell phone rings. She picks it up from the table and answers the call.

Alakemefa: Hello, please who am I speaking with? [The network is breaking.] Hello, please, speak up a bit. I can't hear you. Hello o! I can barely hear you.

F.R.S.C Officer: Am calling from the Federal Road Safety Commission Accident and Emergency Hospital. Am I speaking with Mrs. Alakemefa?

Alakemefa: Yes, what's it?

F.R.S.C Officer: I'm sorry to inform you that your husband was involved in a ghastly automobile accident.

Alakemefa: [Screams] Jesus! Where's he? [Pacing back and forth.]

F.R.S.C. Officer: The accident was so terrible that your husband lost his life. [Alakemefa startles. Her body is shaking terribly]. His corpse is currently deposited at......

Alakemefa: [Shouts at the top of her voice and collapse. Groaning] I'm dead o!

Esther: [Rushes in. Seeing her mother on the floor, her heart beats rapidly. She gasps with surprise at her mother's grief-stricken expression] Mum, mum! What happened? [She draws the closest chair near her and helps her to sit down. Alakemefa is crying inconsolably.] Mum! Please tell me why you're crying. What happened?

Alakemefa: [Tearfully] your dad is dead o-o-o!

Esther: [Mouth flings open in horror and her hand comes up to cover it.] What!? [She couldn't believe her ears. Tears rolling down to her cheeks.] What did you just say? My dad is dead?! How? No, it can't be! [Crying bitterly.] Oho-o-o-o! My only dad is gone! [Both crying] how can I cope with the affairs of life? [Soliloquizing.] Dad, assuming you know, you shouldn't have heeded my plea.

Alakemef: [Crying increases.] Oweilaemi-o-o-o! Oweilaemi-o-o-o! Please come back o-o-o! Come back and amend the broken pieces of my life o! My life is now like a chipped bottle that's no longer recyclable. [Weeping bitterly.] Chai! A great cloud has covered me. My glorious destiny has been shattered by the fiery storms of this world. Oh, God! Why did you allow the cold hands of death to snatch my husband to the land of the dead where no one returns to their loved ones, He's now going to be cold in his grave!

Esther: [Crying intensely] A-a-a-a-ah! Daddy! Why did you leave me behind? The flower you planted in the world is no longer rooted to the ground. I'm now vulnerable to the strong wind of the enemies. Why not take me to that land where I will be forever in the presence of your watchful eye. Oh! Noel must pay for this! Daddy, you wouldn't have gone to the prison. Alas, you are no more.

Alakemefa: [Sobbing] eh-e-e-e! I'm no longer a proud woman. I'm now classified as a widow. I can no longer dare to look into the faces of the scorners. They will now come out as men to claim the legacy you left behind.

Esther: [At this point, rolling on the floor, crying inconsolably.] Aargh! Daddy, I'm truly sorry for what I've caused you! [Sniffles] you lost your life because of me-e-e-e! I will never forgive myself! [Some neighbors enter. Consoling both Alakemefa and Esther.]

2nd Neighbour: [To Alakemefa] Take heart. God knows why. He gives life and takes when he requires. He's the all-knowing God.

1st Neighbour: [To Esther] dou, (sorry) ango kuro mor. (Just put yourself together) because no amount of crying will resuscitate him.

2nd Neighbour: [To Alakemefa] ba you ku mor (stop crying) [pats Alakemefa on the shoulder.] Stop crying sister. [Alakemefa sniffles] God has a predestined time for every human to depart this cruel world to join their forefathers.

1st Neighbour: [To Alakemefa] your husband is resting in Abraham's bosom. Enjoying the peace of the Lord.

2nd Neighbour: [To Esther] my dear, stop crying. You've cried all your eyes out. Crying won't bring him back. God has a purpose for everything. [Esther is still crying] my dear, do you want to cry yourself to sleep? Crying doesn't help to fix things right. It only causes more misfortune. Please listen to me, everything under the sun is for a purpose. Your dad has fulfilled his purpose here on earth that is why he has joined his ancestors.

SCENE THREE

[Esther is lying in bed. She covers herself with a blanket. She's very ill. Shivering seriously beneath the blanket. Alakemefa walks in with a tray of tea and four thick slices of bread.]

Alakemefa: You're lingering in bed all day. [She pulls off the blanket Esther is covering.] Try to get up and eat something.

Esther: [Sits up feebly.] Mum, I can't eat. I have no appetite to eat.

Alakemefa: [Encouraging her to eat.] At least, eat two slices of the bread and wash it down with the tea so that you can take the evening dosages of your medication. Please! [Alakemefa takes a slice of bread, split it into two and gives her a piece to eat. She tries to feed her but Esther declines.]

Esther: Mum, I'm tired. This illness does not respond to medication. This is the third week I'm on medication now. My illness is really getting out of hand. I'm scared.

Alakemefa: [Pats her on the shoulder.] Don't despair, the Lord is our strength. [She weeps silently.] How I wish your dad is still alive.

Esther: [Compassionately] mum it is Ok, stop crying.

Alakemefa: We have been to four different hospitals yet the disease is still unknown. It could have been better if the doctors were able to find out the particular sickness that's debilitating your health.

Esther: Mum! This illness is actually getting on my nerves. I'm fed up with this sickness. The doctors too couldn't be able to trace the source of the sickness. Why are all these happening to me?

Alakemefa: [Feels sad. She smoothens Esther's rough hair.] My daughter, these are just mere temptations. By the grace of God, we will scale through. Don't give up on God because he will never give up on us.

Esther: Mum, you're more than a shield. You never let me down in the test of time. You're the light of my life. In my darkest nights, you always appear with your sparkling light. Mummy, I love you.

Alakemefa: [Gives a glimmer of a smile. Holds her by the hands.] My daughter! You're my world; you are my happiness, you're all I got, you mean everything to me and I will go the extra mile to make sure you're safe and sound. Tomorrow 10:00 a.m. on the dot, we will go to the University of Ojobo Teaching Hospital (UOTH).

Esther: Okay mum! [Alakemefa gives her a light hug and leaves. Esther falls back on the bed and pulls the blanket over her head and sleeps.]

CURTAIN

SCENE FOUR

[Inside the consultant's office, the doctor is sitting on a chair scanning a file. He's wearing a transparent spectacle with thick black frames. He hangs the stethoscope on his neck. The office is beautifully furnished. A poster, depicting how to prevent Lassa fever is hung on the wall. Sphygmomanometer, files, and some books are on the desk. Esther and her mother enter. Esther is dressed in a flowery gown while her mother wears a blouse and a skirt.]

Alakemefa: Good Morning, doctor.

Doctor: Good morning, dear, please take a seat. [Esther and Alakemefa sit opposite the doctor.] How can I help you?

Alakemefa: Ehn, it is close to a month now, my daughter here has been seriously ill. We've gone to different hospitals but no avail. The doctors could not be able to detect the particular sickness that's hampering her health.

Doctor: [Takes off his spectacle.] Young lady, how are you feeling?

Esther: Doctor, I usually feel nauseous and dizzy. If I manage to do mild domestic works, it will always leave me exhausted. There's this constant chronic headache that gets me mad whenever it comes. At times, I do catch a cold.

Doctor: [prying her eyelids open. Puts his stethoscope to her chest]. Your case is a special one [He picks a blue Biro from his lab coat breast pocket, takes a blank sheet of paper and starts writing on it.] She has to go to our medical laboratory technician for a thorough diagnosis [He gives Alakemefa the piece of paper.] Firstly, go to the pharmacy and buy the medicines I've written in this paper. Make sure she takes the medicines right after you've purchased them. It will subside the headache and the cold for the time being.
Alakemefa: Ok, thank you, doctor.

Doctor: You're welcome. [Both Alakemefa and Esther leave. He continues with what he was doing. A female nurse enters.]

Nurse: I'm here sir.
Doctor: Have you administered the oral suspension to the patient at ward eight?

Nurse: Yes sir.

Doctor: Good! Also, give him 3ml of Ceftriaxone injection and 1 ampoule of Artemether injection through intramuscular before you give him the Ciprofloxacin caplet and Lonart tablet. The Ciprofloxacin and Lornart regiment are b d, 8 hourlies... Check his blood pressure first. OK?

Nurse: Okay sir. [She writes the doctor's prescription on the patient's file]

Doctor: Has the paediatrician come?

Nurse: No sir. He hasn't come yet.

Doctor: No problem, I'll phone him and tell him the details. Oh! Lest I forget, please do well to inform the two ladies at the pharmacy that they should check on me by 11:30 a.m.

Nurse: Sir, but how'll I be able to know those ladies? The ladies there are more than two.

Doctor: One person is wearing a blouse and skirt while her daughter is putting on a white flowery gown. [The nurse exits.]

CURTAIN

SCENE FIVE

[Spotlights revealing Esther on stage. She's lying on a two-seater's sofa in the living room, shivering terribly. Alakemefa is sitting beside her. She seems a bit disoriented by Esther's ill health.

Esther: [is deep in thought] God, why is my whole life in absolute misery?

Alakemefa: Esther, do you still feel like throwing up? [She places her right palm on her cheek to check Esther's body temperature either is still high or not.]

Esther: No mum. Is just that I'm feeling dizzy. Mum, I'm worried. I don't know what will become of me. My life is in a state of constant flux. This illness is beyond human comprehension. Why is it that all the doctors we've ever met couldn't be able to detect the cause of my sickness and give me the right medications? I don't know how to get out of this predicament. I'm fed up. Is this life I'm living or is there another? A life I'm not even certain of my tomorrow. A life where all my dreams, hopes and aspirations are now drowned in an ocean of sorrow. A life, vulnerable to anguish and discomfort. I have no father to look up to. My life is now bursting with feelings of unexplainable melancholy. I'm no longer getting comfortable in my own skin. A life where everything is revolving against me. It is over four months now my safe little perfect world went up in smoke. [Tears streaming down her face.]

Alakemefa: [Couldn't control her emotions any longer. She starts sobbing.] My daughter, it is not true that you have lost all hope. [Her face looks gloomy.] Do not despair. Life isn't a funfair but warfare. In essence, we are in a spiritual battle. This your ill-health is as a result of the manipulation of the wicked to truncate your life. We need to engage God in this battle because, with him, the impossible becomes possible. You know what? We are going to meet pastor Ebikeme for fervent prayers tomorrow to know the root cause of this ill-health and God's intervention. Because I firmly believe that when God steps in, the enemies that are afflicting your life will flee.

Esther: Mum, I agree with you. This illness is not ordinary. It is beyond the natural. Imagine, professional doctors like Akpoebi at the University of Ojobo Teaching Hospital couldn't know the cause of this sickness. [She turns her body to change position on the sofa.]

Alakemefa: I have already phoned pastor Ebikeme. He says

tomorrow, by 4 p.m. the church is holding her general prayer meeting. So, we should come and participate. He will utilize that opportunity to urge the church to pray for us. We need to get there on time. It is high time we seek the face of God. [Alakemefa gets up.] Let me go and warm the lou`fi`e so that you can eat lunch. [She pats her on the shoulder gently.] I love you, dearie. [Alakemefa dashes to the kitchen.]

Esther: I love you, mummy. [She tries to sit up and reaches the TV remote control on the table and switches off the television.]

CURTAIN

SCENE SIX

[In the church, a chorister is on the altar, singing praises. Members of the church are still trooping in. The front row is already filled up by early arrivals. The church is beautifully decorated, particularly the altar which cannot be overemphasized. Alakemefa and Esther enter. Esther couldn't pelt along like the other members due to the state of her ill health. An usher comes to her aid and helps her to sit down. Alakemefa sits next to her. The chorister swings into worship which electrifies the atmosphere.]

Chorister: At the centre of it all,
It's you that I see (2×)

There is power in your name
Miracle happen in your name,
As we lift our hands in praise
It's you that I see (2×).
You are bigger,
bigger than the biggest.
You are stronger,
stronger than the strongest.
You are higher,
higher than the highest.
You are greater,
greater than the greatest Jesus (4×).

[Pastor Ebikeme is intensely engrossed with the worship, lifts his hands towards heaven, and speaks in tongues. The majority of the members got carried away by the rhythms of the worship. Some lifting their hands while others are kneeling.] You are greater, greater than the greatest Jesus.... [An officiating minister steps into the altar with a Bible. The chorister stops singing and walks to the choir unit to sit down.]

Officiating Minister: Someone that is glad in God's presence, make a resounding joyful noise unto the Lord! [Exalting the name of the Lord.] He is worthy, awesome, faithful to be praise! The eternal rock of ages, Lord, we thank you. [He flips through the Bible.] You may be seated in God's presence. The word of charge is taken from psalm 34:1-10 [He reads the verses and leaves.

Pastor Ebikeme: [steps into the altar and walks straight away to the pulpit.] Praise thy Lord!

Congregation: Hallelujah!

Pastor Ebikeme: The Holy Spirit just ministered to me that there is someone here, the person's soul encompasses grief and agony. Oh, Sweet Jesus! I will praise your name from the rising of the sun unto the going down of the same. [He worships God] You are God. From beginning to the end.

There is no place for argument.
You are God all by yourself. (2x)
Praise thy Lord!

Congregation: Hallelujah!

Pastor Ebikeme: It is time for intercession. First and foremost, there is a family here I want us to pray for. Sister Alakemefa and Esther step forward to the altar. [Alakemefa holds Esther by the hand, they both gradually move to the altar. Both kneel in front of the altar.] Brethren, let's intercede on behalf of this family. Any gang up of hell contending with this family; pray that by the power of the Holy Ghost, let such forces be destroyed. [Everybody prays].

Esther: [Crashes down the floor and starts rolling rapidly. The evil spirit in her manifests.]

Ho-o-o-o-o-o-o-o! Just let her be. She's mine. She has dedicated her life to me. She belongs to my kingdom.

Alakemefa: [Widens her eyes in amazement.] God forbids! She belongs to God Almighty.

Pastor Ebikeme: You evil spirit, I command you, get out of this body right now! This body is the dwelling place of the Holy Spirit. You have no right to dwell in this body. From the crown of her head to the sole of her feet is covered with the blood of Jesus.

Esther: [Evil spirit in her manifesting.] She entered into a covenant with me that can never be broken.

Pastor Ebikeme: Matthew 16:19 makes me understand that the keys of the kingdom of God have been given unto me: And whatever I bind on earth shall be bound in heaven, and whatever I loose on earth shall be loosed in heaven. Therefore, you evil spirit, I cast you out of her body in the name of Jesus Christ.

Esther: [Screams] I won't leave this body. She's subjected to die. I will torment her until she dies.

Pastor Ebikeme: Christ has redeemed her with his precious blood. You spirit of death, I rebuke you, get out of this body in the name of Jesus! [Esther sleeps off. Pastor Ebikeme calls out.] Sister Alakemefa, please take a seat. [Alakemefa sits down.] The Holy Spirit unveiled to me that your daughter swears an oath with her boyfriend. They sealed it with an exchange of their blood.

Alakemefa: [Hunches forward and stands up from her chair in total disbelief.] My goodness! I can't believe my ears. Pastor, did I hear you right? My daughter, swore an oath with her boyfriend in exchange for their blood?

Pastor Ebikeme: Yes.

Esther: [Flushes her eyelid open, gets up from the floor, and dusts her gown. She moistens her lips with her tongue] Why was I on the floor?

Pastor Ebikeme: [To an usher] Give her a chair to sit down.
[Esther sits down] Humph! Esther, did you swear an oath with your boyfriend?

Esther: [Gives her mother a downcast glance.] Ehm, ehm ---

Alakemefa: My friend, answer the question!

Esther: [Stammers] eh-e-e-e ye- yes!

Alakemefa: [places her hands on her head.] I am finished!
Esther, you have finished me! You swore an oath with your boyfriend. Not only that, you both sealed it with the exchange of your blood.

Pastor Ebikeme: Sister Alakemefa, it's okay. No problem has no solution. You have come to the presence of the Lord. In the presence of the Lord, there's liberty. Esther, how did the whole thing happen?

Esther: Initially, when we started our relationship, we both agreed on a genuine relationship that will lead to marriage without sex. Doubra told me that he does not believe in premarital sex due to celibate reasons. He asked me whether I share his views. I said yes. On the other hand, I had the grand plan to get married as a virgin. premised on these facts, we decided to swear an oath so that we won't betray each other. The oath is on the basis that we should remain faithful to each other until we get married. If anyone cheats on the other person, the person will die.

Alakemefa: Jesus Christ! This girl has finished me o! [Others listening intently shake their heads in astonishment.] I'm shocked to the core. Esther! See what you have gotten yourself into.

Esther: For us to make it concrete, we pierced each other's thumb with a needle. He licked my blood and I also licked his. [She goes on her knees and tearfully.] Mum, I'm truly sorry. I never knew it will turn out this bad. I have cheated on Doubra! [Crying] mum, I didn't cheat on him intentionally. Dear Lord have mercy on me.

Pastor Ebikeme: Is okay. You have asked for forgiveness, so God with his infinite mercies has forgiven you. He has purchased you with His precious blood. But the question is, do you truly love that Doubra and are willing to marry him against all odds? I know you are pretty curious why I ask this question. [Alakemefa raises her right hand to rest her chin on the palm. She listens with keen interest.]

Esther: [Nods her head slowly.] Yes, Sir.

Pastor Ebikeme: My dear, you both made the best decision a good Christian is supposed to make. Marriage is honorable if the bed is undefiled. The only mistake is you both swore an oath which is against the will of God. Jesus speaking in Matthew 5:34. But I say unto you, swear not at all. Being a child of God, it's true you are not supposed to defile the bed before marriage. Nevertheless, the mistake has been done. My candid advice to you as a pastor is; if you want to marry Doubra, you have to tell him the truth that you are no longer a virgin. It's better you open up to him before he finds out.

Esther: [Shyly.] Thanks for your words of encouragement. I will act on them, Sir.

Pastor Ebikeme: Brethren, let's pray for her. [Everyone stretches forth their hands to her direction and both prayed for God's forgiveness and intervention.]

CURTAIN

ACT SIX
SCENE ONE

[Ebitimi is in a melancholy mood. She's sitting on a bench by the window of her house veranda. She looks so confused, thinking about how to bail her son out of prison. All sorts of ideas flash across her mind. All of a sudden, she gets up; takes her phone, and dials Doubra's father.]

Ebitimi: Hello!

Olotuowei: Yes, who's it?

Ebitimi: Is me, Ebitimi. Doubra's mother. I was opportune to collect your phone number from your friend Samuel. I saw him recently for the first time in many years. I bumped into him at the first bank last week Wednesday.

Olotuowei: Oh, that's great! How's he doing?

Ebitimi: He's doing good. It's been ages. How is work?

Olotuowei: Work is good. Hum, what persuades you to call me today? I thought you've forgotten me completely. Ever since we our marriage ended in divorce, you never intended to call me. Why today? Moreover, the last time I checked, this year makes it 25 years since we went our separate ways and it wasn't your habit to ask about my wellbeing. Why now?

Ebitimi: Actually, I was contemplating all day to call and tell you the predicament your first son Doubra is into. I beseech you, let's cast away our flaws and join hands to help our son out of the ugly situation he's into. Please.

Olotuowei: [Gives a deep sigh through the phone.] Hum, after a couple of years, you just pop out of the blue and want me to help your son out of an ugly situation. The son that you snatched from me long ago. Now, you're expecting me to help him. [Hangs up the call.]

Ebitimi: [feeling a bit despondent and helpless; moving back and forth, thinking about the appropriate step to take. Paibi enters] Thank God you are here. How warming it is to see you.

Paibi: Good evening ma!

Ebitimi: Evening my son. How're you doing?

Paibi: I'm doing fine ma'am. Ma, you look tense up. Are you still worried that Doubra is in prison? Don't stress yourself much. Very soon, he will be out of that horrible place.

Ebitimi: When? My son when? See the awkward predicament your friend has gotten himself into. Where would I have the money to bail him out of prison now? I have exhausted all my money on his academic expenditures.

Paibi: I understand. Cast away your worries. It’s just a matter of time, sooner or later, the police will set him free, just rely on God, [He sits on the bench] I just come to check on you to know how you’re faring?

Ebitimi:Thank you, my son. You're one in a million. Your kind of friend is rare. [She sits on the bench next to him.] Ehn, I called Doubra's father not too long to help me bail Doubra out of prison but he is mad at me because since our marriage ended in divorce and I left with Doubra without his approval, he doesn't want to hear any version of the story I intended to tell him. He hung up on me. Since Doubra's father and I split up, I've been raising Doubra alone. It's just that I'm quite financially down that is why I needed his support ... [Ebitimi phone rings.] He is the one calling. [She answers the call] Hello!

Olotuowei: I just realized that it will do us no good if we keep on with this attitude of depriving each other of our responsibility as a father and mother. Certainly, the negative impact of our split up is affecting our children. So, I have decided to cast aside all the mistakes we both have made for the sake of our children. Now tell me, what's the ugly situation our son is into?

Ebitimi: First and foremost, I want to thank you for your understanding. To be sincere, I'm also at fault for abandoning my obligation as a mother all this while. In brief, your son Doubra was arrested, he is now in the custody of police in my community district police headquarter.

Olotuowei: What? What did he do?

Ebitimi: To cut long story short, he was kidnapped and released after three days. He noticed who masterminded the kidnap, the bastard came and arrested Doubra in my own house for tarnishing his image as a kidnapper. And on the other hand, he has no proof to validate the fact that it was the guy that kidnapped him.

Olotuowei: I have heard you. Just tell me your house address. I'll be there before the morning sun goes down tomorrow.

Ebitimi: No. 14 Owei road; Opposite Johnson car wash, Tuomo.

Olotuowei: Okay. I'll be there tomorrow.

Ebitimi: Thanks. I'm grateful. I do appreciate your concern.

Olotuowei: You're welcome.

CURTAIN

SCENE TWO

[In the police station, a police constable is flipping through a rap sheet placed in a stiff frame on top of a desk. Olotuowei and Ebitimi enter. Olotuowei is dressed in a blue well-fitted suit that accentuates his enchanting personality and black Italian pair of shoes which depicts he is a man of integrity and influence.

Constable: Good morning.

Olotuowei: Morning officer.

Constable: How may I help you, Sir?

Olotuowei: Firstly, I want to bail my son Doubra. Secondly, I want to know who arrested my son and lastly why he was arrested?

Constable: Please, take a seat, Sir. [Pointing at the direction of the chairs.] Let me go through the blotter to find out his details.

Olotuowei: Ok, please do. [Both Olotuowei and Ebitimi sit down. The police constable takes the blotter and flips through it. The D.P.O walks in. His eyes catch Olotuowei.]

D.P.O: Gracious me! Hon. Olotuowei!

Olotuowei: Oh, my goodness! Officer James. [Both shake hands.] It's a real pleasure to meet you.

D.P.O: Pleasure is mine.

Olotuowei: It's been a while. Where have you been?

D.P.O: On the surface of the earth. [Both laugh] Being a police officer, is like a dice that rolls in different directions. So, here I found myself. By the grace of God, I am the head of this division.

Olotuowei: That's divine!

D.P.O: Why are you here?

Olotuowei: Someone kidnapped my son and tortured him for three consecutive days because of a girl my son is dating. [D.P.O makes himself comfortable on a chair.] After he sets him free, he still stirred up the courage to arrest my son for tarnishing his reputation.

D.P.O: Oh, that boy! Ehm, [Stammers] Dou... Dou... Doubra is your son?

Olotuowei: Yes.

D.P.O: Really? So sorry, I didn't know he is your son. I will send one of the police to release him right away.

Olotuowei: I will be eternally grateful. On a more serious note, I want to know that godforsaken bastard who has the guts to kidnap my son. Not only that, he went ahead to arrest him. I'm desperate to press charges against him for his outrageous acts.

D.P.O: Noted Sir. [Pulling his legs]. You haven't changed. You still do put up your authoritative attitude.

Ebitimi: [Smiles] He's known as a man of authority. [Both laughs.]

D.P.O: [Calls out the police constable.] Bright!

Constable: Sir!

D.P.O: Suspend whatever thing you are doing and go straight away to release the boy that was arrested for sullying someone's reputation. Also, make sure you phone the guy that put him behind bars that I need his presence now. He should come over without delay.

Constable: Okay Sir! [He exits]

D.P.O: Hon. Olotuowei, in the light of what you were saying, do you think pressing charges against the guy in question is the best decision?

Olotuowei: Yes of course. That nonentity kidnapped my son. He must not go scot-free. He must face the law. I was told that my son was in those kidnapper's custody for three consecutive days. He was given neither food nor water. He nearly died in the process.

Ebitimi: Yes, it is true.

D.P.O: Those boys are hardhearted. [The police constable returns shortly with Doubra. Ebitimi stands up and hugs him tightly, shedding tears.]

Doubra: Mum it is ok-eh! Stop crying. At least, they have released me. [The D.P.O disengages Ebitimi from Doubra.]

D.P.O: Why are you crying? I reckon that you should thank God that he is alive. [The Police constable offers Doubra a chair] Please sit down and have some rest.

Doubra: [Sits down] Mum, I truly appreciate your effort. In thick and thin, you haven't let me down. Your love towards me cannot be quantified. Indeed, mothers are priceless. You can't buy one in the supermarket.

Olotuowei: My son, Doubra! [Down in the mouth.] I am sincerely sorry.

Doubra: [Surprised.] I don't understand, what are you saying?

Olotuowei: [Voice dwindles] I am your father.

Doubra: [Gives him a flinty gaze.] My what?! If indeed you are my father, where have you been over these donkeys of years? [He feels dispirited.] Where were you when I was facing the rigors of life in this world? No, you can't be my father!

Ebitimi: I know you will find it difficult to comprehend the fact that he is your father. But I want you to find a place in your heart to forgive him. You know, we are all imperfect in the sight of God. We are all human beings. We have flaws. In essence, I also did not perform my obligation as a mother to your younger ones. Please, temper justice with mercy, I beg you. Forgiveness is the needle that knows how to mend.

Doubra: [Becomes sympathetic.] But at least, he would have shown up occasionally.

Olotuowei: I am really sorry. It wasn't intentional. I was overwhelmed with aggression.

D.P.O: My dear, I don't have much to say, all I have to say is please forgive your father. To err is human and to forgive is divine. Let bygones be bygones. [Alakemefa and Esther enter. As soon as they enter, Doubra just spotted Esther.]

Doubra: [Whelms with a rush of joy.] Esther dearie!

Esther: [Rushes down to catch up with him.] Oh my gosh! You are out!

Doubra: [Rushes along to meet her.] Yes!

Esther: [Plants a kiss on his forehead.] I am so happy to see you. [Alakemefa exchanges pleasantries with everyone].

Ebitimi: [To Olotuowei] This is Esther's mother, Alakemefa.

Olotuowei: My in-law! How are you doing?

Alakemefa: [Smiling] Fine Sir. And you?

Olotuowei: I'm doing good. Your daughter is indeed a beautiful handiwork of God's finest creature. She is a replica of her mother. [Alakemefa smiles] Now I understand why my son can't do without her. [Doubra smirking]

D.P.O: [Teasing] To be frank, your daughter is exceptionally beautiful! She is fair to look upon. [Kidding] Do you still have another beautiful damsel? I want to hook her up to my beloved son. [Both laugh]

Olotuowei: You never cease to amaze me!

[Laughing dies down. Alakemefa winks at Esther as a signal to tell Doubra their motive for coming to the station. Esther understands the signal and craves for everyone's indulgence for the confession she wants to make. Everybody was amazed at her sudden change of attitude. Her attitude so whelmed them that they are stunned into silence. Everybody is curious to hear what she has to say. She holds Doubra's hands, tears flooding down her face like a rapid flow of an ocean. She goes on her knees, sniffling. She lost control of her emotions. Doubra couldn't help to control his emotions either.]

Doubra: You are making me nervous and miserable. What is going on? [Everyone in the station watches in awe and wonder.] What on earth have you done?

Esther: [Tearfully] I have betrayed your trust.

Doubra: What do you mean by that?

Esther: I have broken the vow! The oath we both took.

Doubra: [Exceedingly angry] w-h-a-t?! Do you mean you have been cheating on me all this while?

Esther: No! I can explain.

Doubra: [Aggressively] explain what?! How you have been cheating on me? How foolish I am to believe in all the fairy tales of everlasting love.

Ebitimi: Erhhh! Tebra! Wonders shall never cease! [She lingers in the station, putting her palms together.] You both took an oath? Chai! Doubra, I am highly disappointed in you. Do you know the gravity of swearing an oath? Do you know the adverse effect if anyone deviates?

Doubra: [Angrily.] Mummy! Please, stop! Esther, I trusted you. How could you betray me? Despite the unimaginable love I have for you, is this what I get in return? So, it is true that love is just a mere emotion that controls our actions. Love blindfolds the eyes not to see the reality unfolding itself. Oblivious of the dangers springing up. So, it is true that love deafens the ears to the extent that you don't even listen to those you cherish in your life except the words that of your love. [Sobbing] so my mummy was right when she said she is no longer in support of our relationship. Because she senses the dangers springing up. I was actually blindfolded by love to see the fact that your next-door neighbour is truly your boyfriend.

Esther: [Crying] No! It is not true!

Doubra: My mum was right. I would have stuck to her decision. I was just a lonely man looking for love.

Alakemefa: [Looks sad] Doubra and Ebitimi, I know that my daughter has done wrong. Doubra, she didn't betray you intentionally. She is just a victim of circumstance. Not only my daughter but also myself [Hitting her chest with her right palm.] Is not an exception. If she doesn't love you, we wouldn't have come here. Only God knows what my daughter and I have passed through because of the oath you both took. She nearly lost her life. Esther told me everything that had happened between you, Noel, and herself. That boy Noel pushed Esther over the edge. He had been pestering her to date him of which she declined. One faithful day, my husband and I weren't in the house. We both travelled. It rained heavily that very day. The rain fury destroyed his apartment roof so he came to our house for shelter. According to her, she was got carried away and before she knew what was going on, she found herself making love with him. In the heat of the moment, she turned to ice and dance to the beat of her own drum. She has been a virgin all her life until she lost her virginity to him that very day. It was Noel that deflowered her. And that was the last day she ever had an affair with someone. He, realizing that she was a virgin, wants to date her by all means of which she didn't give him the chance. That's why all these kidnapping issues and the likes come up. Moreover, my daughter fell terribly ill as a result of breaking the vow. She nearly lost her life in the process. As a result of her ill health, she stopped schooling. We went to several hospitals but to no avail. After all efforts proved abortive, I took her to my pastor for prayers and God's intervention but only to discover you two swore an oath. My heart beats rapidly behind the walls of my chest when my pastor told me that you both swore an oath in exchange for your blood. Because swearing an oath is not a child's play. Furthermore, my daughter pleaded with her dad to bail you out of prison because she loves you and wants you out of prison. My husband, [crying] God bless his soul! On his way to bail you out of prison, died in an auto crash. [She wrinkles her nose in disgust and sniffles.] Oh, death! How mean you are? I am now…

Ebitimi: [Cuts in] Oh my! Do you mean your husband is late?

Alakemefa: [Wiping her dripping tears with her bare palms.] Y-e-s! Those were dark times in my family. I got into a stew of unexpected emotions.
After my husband died, Esther's world fell apart and she went into a tailspin.

Doubra: Oh my God! This is bad! He lost his life because of me! Ma'am, I am truly sorry. Accept my condolence.

Alakemefa: It's okay.

Olotuowei: [Clears his throat.] Hmm, first of all, I express my sincere condolence. We've heard what you just said. There is no doubt that your daughter, truly loves my son. But the point I want to figure out is she shouldn't have allowed the boy to come so close to her, talk more of having an affair with him. Bearing it in mind that the guy in question is pestering her to date him. He is not a drum! It is only drums that are given the sound beating that produces beautiful rhythms. Sexual control is like a kerosene lamp. If you do not manage the wick properly, the flame will leap too high, the glass will be darkening with smoke and the lamp will give no light. You have to adjust the wick to give proper light. Now you can see what this singular mistake has resulted in. You don't allow your emotions to control you. Rather, you control your emotions. You allowed your emotions to override your voice of reasoning. You would have built a brick wall around your emotions. You and I know the adverse effect of swearing an oath. [Timipere and Noel enter. Both holding each other's hands, chatting and laughing. Immediately they enter, Olotuowei eyes catch them. He is thrown into confusion. He is surprised to see Ebi in the station.] Hey! Ebi, what are you doing here?

Noel: [Couldn't believe his eyes, seeing Ebitimi, Esther, Alakemefa, Doubra, and his father in the station.] Dad!

Doubra: [Wrapped in anger, rushes down to interrogate Noel, oblivious of what is going on.] You piece of trash! Do you think you can rip me off? [He seizes his shirt. Ebitimi dashes Noel with a hard slap on the face. D.P.O is trying to separate them.]

Olotuowei: [Confused.] Ebitimi, what is going on?

Ebitimi: He's the one that arrested Doubra.

Olotuowei: [Looks skeptical.] What! [He gives Noel a dirty slap.] My own son! Capable of doing all this rubbish?

Ebitimi: [Stares at him in utter disbelief.] Your son? Wait for a second, do you mean this meathead is your son?

Olotuowe: [Downhearted.] Yes! He is our son. I never knew the chump in question will turn out to be our son? [Noel, rolling his eyes. He feels goose pimples erection. He is surprised to hear that Ebitimi is his mother because he could vividly remember the inimical attitude, he gave her when he went to arrest Doubra.] This is Ebi! Doubra's immediate younger brother. I did not know he bears Noel as a name.

Ebitimi: Aargh! God, why? [She is heartsick to learn of their divorce.] Why is everything turning upside down?

Noel: [Bursts into tears.] What a small world! I never knew that I was doing all these terrible things to my blood brother. The brother I've been longing to see for the past couple of years. My heart swells with a sea of tears to realize that I pushed my own mother onto the floor. [Doubra gives him an inimical glare.] Ooh! So, I was being hostile to my blood brother. The brother I have been searching all over for.

Doubra: [In dismay, falls down on the floor. Perspiring profusely. Realizing that his worst enemy in the world turns out to be his blood brother. Olotuowei helps him to sit down on the chair. Esther wipes the perspiration from his forehead with her handkerchief.] Mummy and daddy! I hope you both have seen what your split-up has resulted in? [Both Olotuowei and Ebitimi look downcast.] What a tragedy your divorce has caused. Now, you don't even know your biological son because of your greed and selfishness. [Tears coursing down Ebitimi's cheeks. Olotuowei is moved to tears.] Mummy! Is this not the brother I have been craving to see each day that passes by? Because you refused to tell me the truth from the onset, my worst enemy in the universe turns out to be my only brother I have been longing to see over these donkeys of years. It pains me so much to realize that this scallywag turns out to be the brother I was looking for.

Esther: [Crying silently. The only person that had an affair with her happens to be a brother to her fiancé. She taps Doubra's shoulder tenderly] Dear, it is okay! God knows why things are going this way. Maybe, we are not meant for each other. We have to accept our fate. At last, you have seen your brother. The brother you told me that you can't wait to see when the right time comes. [Sobbing.] He happens to be the one that deflowered me. My life is now like chaff. The precious part had been tampered with. I need to stay out of your life and amend the broken pieces of my life. Because life is not always going to turn out the way we expect; every day is a new adventure.

Doubra: [Overwhelms with emotions.] This is the most important day of my life. And you are an integral part of my being. Please don't leave me. I want you to stay. You know I do love you. Come hell or high water. I will forever love you.

[All this while, Timipere is in a sober mood, her face is clouded with sorrow and shame. She buries her face in her arms.]

Ebitimi: [Sniffles with teary eyes and sighs slowly.] I never knew divorce is accompanied by such great consequences. Because of aggression, I abandoned my role as a mother, not bearing in mind I have another son elsewhere. Now, he looks as vicious as a wild cat. My own son came to my house and pushed me down on the floor, not knowing that he is hurting his mother. What a world! Things wouldn't have been in this mess if Doubra and Ebi knew that they were brothers. Oh! What a great catastrophe that has befallen us!

Two blood brothers are desperately in love with one particular girl, oblivious of the fact that they are brothers.

[The D.P.O. is amazed about the drama that is going on.]

Olotuowei: [Sighs heavily.] Doubra! I am truly sorry. I am short of words to express my innermost feelings of how sorry I am. I was ignorant to the truth that split up is not the best decision about a cracking marriage, rather you make an amendment. This is just a clear picture of the disadvantages of a divorce. On the other hand, your brother Ebi, though you people called him Noel, his actual name from birth is Ebi. Your brother has offended me greatly. This is not the way I raised him. I didn't know he will be capable of accusing someone wrongly and arrest the fellow talk more of hiring boys to kidnap you. Ebi, I am so much disappointed in you. See what your inhuman actions have generated. You said that you prefer business to school. I gave you all a caring father is supposed to give his son. Did you know, that it cost me a fortune to establish that well-stock electronic store and still bought a brand-new car for you? I gave you liberty! Peace of mind! Name it! Is this how you are behaving? Lavishing the money on unnecessary things. So, you are this mean and unreasonable! You have turned into a monster, right? I'm going to strip you of your privileges.

Noel: [Crying] Dad! I'm sorry!

Olotuowei: [Aggressively.] Sorry for yourself! You fool! I regret to have you as my son. Come on, give me the car keys! [He snatches the car key from him.] Where are the store keys?

Noel: [Dips a hand inside his trouser pocket and fetches out the bunch of keys and hands it to his father.] Daddy, please I am so sorry. [He kneels, pleading.]

Olotuowei: [Pushes Noel violently.] Go to hell! You fool! From today henceforth, that electronic store at Bomadi market is no longer yours. D.P.O.! Detain this my son Noel, for all his inhuman actions toward his brother.

D.P.O: Okay. Officer John!

Officer John: Sir!

D.P.O: [Pointing a hand at Noel.] Put this young man behind bars.

Officer John: Okay sir! [He drags Noel to the cell.]

Olotuowei: Thank you very much D.P.O. for your understanding. My sincere apologies for the inconveniences. We have caused a lot of commotion in this station. If you are not an understanding friend, you would have chased us out. Once again thank you. I'm eternally grateful.

D.P.O: Don't mention. What are friends for? You are my very good friend. We both have gone a long way.

Olotuowei: My son Doubra, I know I haven't played any part in your life. I want you to understand that I was overwhelmed with aggression. I promise you; I am ready to sponsor you to any length of your academic pursuit. [He brings out a check book from his bag and writes a check of #20,000,000 and gives it to Doubra.] Take this money to buy a car and a suitable house for yourself. You're now the C.E.O. of my company. I want you to start work this month end.

Doubra: [Surprised.] Oh my God! Thank you, Sir. I am very grateful. I don't know how to express how grateful I am right now. Indeed, you have changed my world!

Olotuowei: [writes a check of #500,000 and gives it to Esther.] Take this to continue your education.

Esther: [Astonished.] Gracious me! All this for me? [Jumping for joy.] Thank [stammers] thank... thank you, Sir!

Olotuowei: Just thank God. I sincerely appreciate the genuine love you both have for each other. Love is a unifying factor for a peaceful existence. I give my blessings in this relationship. When you both are done with school, I will solely sponsor your wedding.

You two are a perfect match! You too will make a beautiful couple. I like your union.

Doubra: Thank you, Sir. I truly appreciate the love you have shown to us. I am not taking it for granted. I do understand that we all are humans. I'm also sorry for the way I reacted earlier. Frankly speaking, you don't know how happy I am right now to have such an enchanting and respectful person like you as my father. Today is indeed the happiest day of my life.

Timipere: [Walks up to Esther, tears coursing down her cheeks.] Esther, I'm so sorry-e-e! I am sorry for my hostile attitude towards you. I know, I don't worth being forgiven but I want you to search for a place in your heart and forgive me.

Esther: I'm still not talking to you. How could you do that?

Doubra: Oh dear! Don't be so uptight! Let's kick the past right in the teeth and move on. You don't keep up a price in friendship.

Esther: For the love of God, I've forgiven you.

Timipere: [Tearfully.] Thanks, dear!

Esther: You are welcome. [Drying her tears] come on, put a smile on your face. The prettiest thing you can wear is to smile. I've forgiven you from the depth of my heart.

Olotuowei: [To Esther] My daughter, come and hug me [Esther hugs him. Doubra joins them. Both laughing and smiling. Ebitimi and Alakemefa hug themselves. Olotuowei shakes the D.P.O. for the love he has shown. Olotuowei and Ebitimi embrace themselves, flashing their teeth to show a sign of happiness.]

CURTAIN

SCENE THREE

[Two weeks later, in Mrs. Alakemefa's house. Esther is seen visibly worried in the sitting room.]

Alakemefa: [Enters and sits beside her] How have you been my love?

Esther: [Face looks puzzled] I'm not good mum! It seems like I have missed my period.

Alakemefa: [In fluster] Seriously? How have you been feeling?

Esther: I'm feeling nauseous accompanied by headache and fatigue. My breast feels fuller and heavier. They are tenderly swollen.

Alakemefa: [Disquieted] These are symptoms of early pregnancy. Esther, you are pregnant!

Esther: [Startles] w-h-a-t! I'm what? [Anguished with sorrow] pregnancy is the last word I want to hear mum. [Tears forming in her eyes. Emotionally] I can't believe this mum.

Alakemefa: [With teary eyes, cuddles her tenderly] my daughter, panic not. Be resolute to go through this. Do not allow this pregnancy to weigh you down. You have to accept your fate.

Esther: [Sorrowfully] mum, if truly I'm pregnant, I'm not going to keep this baby because the baby wants to shatter my life. I can't stand it because everything in my life is now falling in place. I'm now thinking of having a blissful married life with Doubra, the love of my life. Peradventure I'm pregnant, it will certainly wreck my marriage plan with Doubra. Oh, dear Lord, I don't want my relationship with Doubra in ruins.

Alakemefa: [Patting her shoulder] don't worry my love. God is in control. I want you to buy a pregnancy test strip [P.T. strip] to ascertain either you are pregnant or not.

Esther: Okay mum. I pray it shouldn't be positive because I can't afford to be pregnant for that fool "Noel", who almost truncates my life. [Takes a deep breath] I can't just bear it!

Alakemefa: [Looks at her with cheerful beaming eyes] what can I do to make you smile my dear daughter. [Smoothing her hair] do you care for some fried Okpoku?

Esther: [Face brightens] yes mum. I will really love it. [Smiles] mum, hearing the word pregnancy took every bone in me but your beaming face sets my fears at rest.

Alakemefa: [Laughs softly] all right then, let me go and get you some from the microwave.

Esther: Okay mum. [Alakemefa dashes off to the kitchen.] Lights fade and return shortly. Later in the day, Alakemefa and Esther are seen busy in the living room. Esther has bought the pregnancy test strip (P.T. Strip)

Alakemefa: [Cuts off the edge of the P.T. Strip pack with a scissors to unveil the strip and inserts it into a small plastic container, containing urine. After about five minutes, she brings it out. To her amazement, it shows two red lines which signify positive] Esther! [Crumbles onto a chair]. The unexpected has happened. [Hands on her head]. You are pregnant!

Esther: [Gasps with regret as tears well up in her eyes] what did you s-a-y? did you just say that I'm pregnant? [Tears dripping from her eyes] mum, I can't have this baby. Not like this, not under this condition. [Whimpering] I can't have this baby fully knowing that it will jeopardize my education as well as my courtship with Doubra [sadly] mum.

Alakemefa: Yes, dear.
Esther: I need you to help me. [sobbing] I want to abort this baby.

Alakemefa: [Sternly] No, no, no, Esther, don't say that! No, no way, you are not aborting this pregnancy. Esther, you are not alone, you can count on me. I promise you; I will help you scale through this.

Esther: Mum I'm sorry to say this. I can't give birth to a baby whom the father is a brother to my fiancé [face looks gloomy] I can't give birth to a baby I didn't even prepare for.

Alakemefa: [Displeased with the idea of terminating the pregnancy] Oh my dear daughter, please do not abort this baby. I beg you. You want to make the greatest mistake in your life. We all know that abortion has virtually claimed millions of lives. You want to kill an innocent child. Abortion is against the will of God. I don't want you to leave me. [Sobbing] you are the only one I have to call a family. Please stay by my side.

Esther: Mum, I do understand but this pregnancy wants to put my life in jeopardy.

Alakemefa: Let me tell you a true-life story. In the western part of Nigeria to be precise Ogun State, where a friend of mine hails from, it's believed that for every wrong act there is always a reward. A couple was faced with such a situation of choosing whether to keep an unwanted foetus because they did not plan to have a baby anytime soon. They were advised by an elder to just keep the baby and see what happens later on. But they did not heed to that, they decided to remove the foetus. Few months after the removal of the foetus, the man lost his job and, on his way, back home he had an accident and died on the spot. Spiritualists say that the gods took his life for taking the life of his own child and the wife should be happy that hers was not taken. Imagine how a woman lost a child and a husband just because of a silly decision. Moreover, the Holy book states clearly that children are of God and what so ever is of God is a blessing to the world. So, my dear daughter, please, for God's sake, do me this favour to keep the baby.

Esther: I have heard you, mum.

Alakemefa: Hmm, let me go to Optimal Health's pharmacy to get you some drugs. Ya alagha fa ti`mi bo me`ne [She leaves for the pharmacy. Lights fades and fully returned]

Esther: [Holding a plastic bottle of an herbal mixture, whimpering] God forgive me for this evil act I'm about to do now. I know, I want to kill an innocent child but I can't give birth to a baby I don't love, cherish and plan for. The baby will definitely suffer. [Tears rolling down from her eyes to her checks] God forgive me. I have to terminate this pregnancy [She slowly drinks the herbal mixture and frowns] Ah, it is too bitter. [She drinks again] what a bitter mixture [About five minutes later, she feels stomach cramps] Ouch! What is happening to me? [Hands on the stomach, groaning in pains] Ow! Ah-a-a-a-a [she clumps onto the floor, rolling with pains, screaming, her voice is too faint to be heard. Her mouth develops foams].

Alakemefa: [Enters, seeing Esther struggling for death on the floor, she screams at the top of her voice as she flings the drugs and holds Esther. Crying inconsolably, shaking Esther seriously. Neighbors rush in. Alakemfa glances and holds the herbal mixture bottle and drops it] Esther! Esther, don't do this to me [Shaking her vigorously] Esther please don't leave me. Why are you doing this to your poor mother?

Neighbor 1: Let's rush her to the hospital.

Neighbor 2: Someone should quickly call an ambulance. [To neighbor 3] hurry, hurry [they hold her up.]

Neighbor 3: Don't block the airway, allow ventilation to enter the house. [To Neighbor 2] I have called an ambulance. The ambulance is on the way. It will soon get here. [Alakemefa howling in terror.]

Neighbor 1: Stop crying. Nothing bad will happen to her. She will be fine. [Esther becomes motionless and lifeless. She gives up the ghost. Alakemefa realizing that Esther has passed on, screams and faints. Within a couple of minutes, the ambulance arrives. On the arrival of the ambulance, the neighbors take Esther to the ambulance.

Alakemefa: [Wakes up, her body is shaking] where is my daughter?

Neighbor 3: We know that it is not easy to lose a daughter and husband within a space of five months, just take heart.

[Alakemefa rushes outside]. She sees Doubra standing opposite the ambulance. She runs to meet him.

Doubra: [To the ambulance officers] I say bring her out of the ambulance!

Ambulance Officer 1: But she is already dead.

Doubra: [Angrily] I know, please bring her out of the ambulance and go your way. I've got this strong conviction in my heart that she is not dead [snivelling] she promised me that she will stay with me forever. [Alakemefa meets him, wailing]

Alakemefa: Oh, mekpo akpo! Esther fede yo-o-o! My only hope is gone! Your brother has finally killed my only daughter! Oh-o-o—o!

Doubra: [Tensed up hearing the words his brother killed his fiancée] hmm, ma is okay! Stop crying. She's not dead.

Ambulance officer 2: [Surprised] see this wise fool! Somebody dead for an hour already. Are you insane? [To ambulance officer1] don't mind this man. Get in and let's leave here.

Doubra: [Angrily] I said, drop her! Don't you understand simple English?

Alakemefa: [Surprised] do you mean Esther my daughter, can come back to life?

Doubra: Yes, ma! She promised to marry me.

Alakemefa: Yes! But she is dead already.

Doubra: No! She is not. She promised to stay with me until death takes us both together to the silent world. [Bystanders watch them in amazement] she promised me that her love for me will last forever like the sun and not even death can cut short that love. [Bystanders murmuring among themselves]

Ambulance Officer 2: Don't mind this dupe! Have you ever seen a dead person come back to life before? [To ambulance officer 1] just get in and let's leave this place now!

Doubra: [Lies in front of the ambulance] you must not leave until you leave her behind. [Everybody is surprised.]

Neighbor 2: She's already dead. Please let them take her to the mortuary.

Doubra: She's not dead. She is still breathing. She is just sleeping.

Ambulance officer 1: [Vexed] let's drop the corpse and leave this lousy place. [They drop Esther's corpse on the ground and zooms off.]

Doubra: [Breaks down and weeps beside the corpse] Oh, what a sweet sorrow! [He holds her by the hand] Please, turn back the heart you've turned away. Give back your kissing breath. Leave not my love as you have left the broken heart of yesterday. But wait, be still, don't lose this way, accept my love and live for today.

Olotuowei: [Taps Doubra's shoulder] my son!

Doubra: Dad! [Surprised seeing his father]

Olotuowei: I know that you love her but she's dead already and she won't come back to life again. I know it's very painful to lose someone very dear to you.

Doubra: [sobbing] Day, she promised to marry me.

Olotuowei: [Looks sad] Son, just take heart. [Helping Doubra to stand up] you have to summon courage to move on with life. It's saddened my heart that despite the pains she went through for your sake, she did not leave to enjoy the benefits of a blissful marriage. And as for Ebi, He will rot in jail for his inhumane actions towards you and..... [tears rolling down to his cheeks] Ah! Ebi will face my wrath. [To Alakemefa] please, accept my sincere condolences. I know that it was my son, No... Noe [stammers] Ebi's heart wrenching actions that led to her death. And I will make sure he suffers in jail. [He takes Esther's corpse to mortuary.]

Doubra: [crying in terror] How I wish this is not happening.

THE END

ABOUT THE AUTHOR

Brisibe Tamarauekiye

Obtained a Bachelor of Science degree in Human Kinetics and Health Education from the University of Port Harcourt, Choba, Nigeria. He's a content creator and a digital marketer. Some of his creative works are Bitter Honey, About Last Night, Mysery Lit, My Past Came Calling, Behind the Scene.